Rodney Peppé

THE MICE AND THE FLYING BASKET

AIR SHOW

LOTHROP, LEE & SHEPARD BOOKS

Other Lothrop picture books by Rodney Peppé

The Kettleship Pirates
The Mice Who Lived in a Shoe

Library of Congress Cataloging in Publication Data

Peppé, Rodney.
   The mice and the flying basket.

   Summary: A family of mice decide to make an airplane
out of a big basket and learn to fly.
   1. Children's stories, English. [1. Mice – Fiction.
2. Flying – Fiction] I. Title.   5|87   E
PZ7.P4212Mg 1985   [E]   84-14360   PEP
ISBN 0-688-04252-X

These are the mice who lived in a shoe. It was a wonderful shoe house.

They earned their living by making baskets for the basket merchant, D. Rat. They made big and small ones, short and tall ones, fat ones, thin ones,

sturdy, flimsy, pretty and plain ones.

But even though everyone in the family worked very hard, D. Rat paid them so little

Ma

Grandma and Grandpa

D. Rat

Ann

that they never had enough money for food.

One day they were so hungry that they began thinking of other ways to earn a living.

Pip, who had seen the Air Show, suggested,
"Why don't we build a flying basket?"

"That's a wonderful idea!" exclaimed Pa, and everyone agreed, except Ma.
"We might win first prize in the Flying Circus," said Sue.
"That's where the money is," said Grandpa, nodding wisely.

So Pa, Grandpa, Pip and Sue went to the Aero Club for advice.
Two brothers called Orville and Wilbur gave them an instruction book, a battery, three motors and some wire.

The next day they set to work. Grandma read out the instructions from Orville and Wilbur's book.

Pa fixed the forward motor while Mick put on the propeller – backwards at first!

Grandpa and Sue assembled the helicopter blades, and Pip made a ladder from the battery wires.

The whole family helped to build the deck — except Ma, who arranged the flags.

Then they built a second basket and attached it to the first. Tim helped to make the wheels.

At last they started to build the wings and tail. Mary switched on the motor, which was naughty!

Pa fixed the rear motor and small propeller.
Ann helped with that. Ma finished her knitting.

The basket was soon ready to fly. There were
seats on deck – the one with the cushion was Ma's.

Orville and Wilbur came to look at the result. "I don't remember baskets in our book," Orville murmured.

"Will you teach us to fly now?" Pa asked them.

First Orville gave Pa another book. This one was called *The Right Way to Fly*.
"It explains everything," said Orville.
"Almost everything," agreed Wilbur.

Then the flying lesson began.
"First thing you do," said Orville, climbing into the pilot's seat, "is switch on the engine."
The flying basket began to move forward.

"There's really nothing to it," shouted Orville.
"Nothing," agreed Wilbur, "unless you count
looping the loop and wing-walking."
The flying basket flew up high in the sky.

After some shaky starts, Ma nearly losing her hat and Tim falling out, the mice learned to fly.

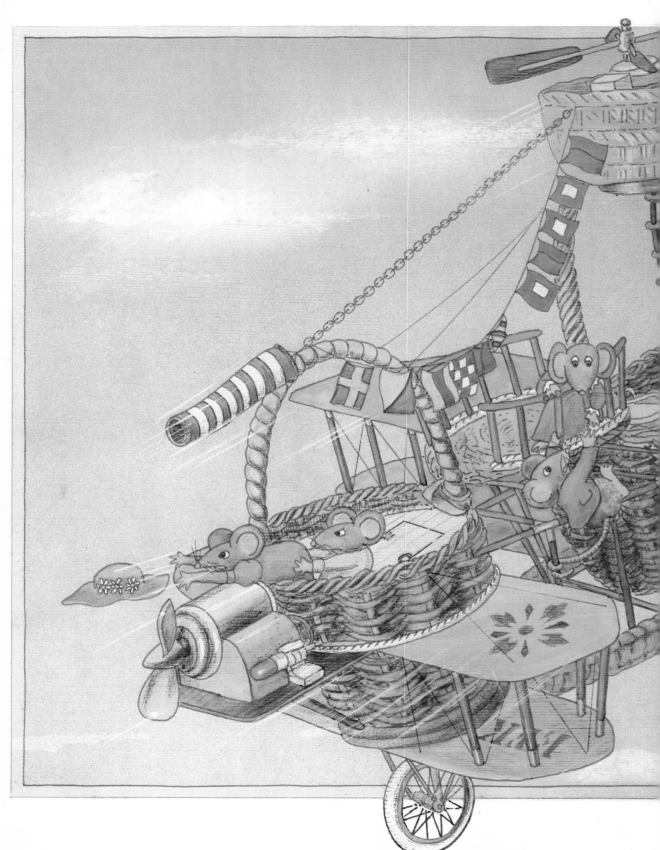

Soon they became so good that they even tried
a few tricks from Orville and Wilbur's book.

At last the day of the Flying Circus arrived. Everyone laughed as the mice piloted their flying basket down the runway.

Then all eyes turned to the Flying Fiend, Baron von Rathoven. His flying dart had a nasty habit of crashing into other aircraft.

When the flying basket took to the air, the mice performed wonderfully, looping the loop.

Suddenly the mice saw Baron von Rathoven coming right at them.

Pip switched the plane into reverse, and the
Rat Baron missed them by a whisker!

The rat and his dart flew out of control and crashed into a muddy pond –

splosh!

The mice heard his cries and flew to the rescue.

They hovered above and threw the rat a rope.

When the miserable von Rathoven was safely aboard, he removed his helmet and goggles. The family gasped.

"It's not the Rat Baron at all!" squeaked Pip.

"It's D. Rat in disguise," shouted the others.
The drenched, dirty rat coughed up muddy
water and shrugged.

"Dangerous driving doesn't pay," said Pa.

The crowd booed slimy D. Rat and cheered as the mice were awarded first prize. Loudest of all were the cheers of Orville and Wilbur.

"You must share the prize," said Pa to Orville and Wilbur. "Then you'll be able to build a flying machine of your own."

D. Rat still dresses up as Baron von Rathoven, but really he's only the ticket-seller for the mice, showing off their famous flying basket. He pretends that he built it himself, but no one ever believes him.